D[ILY]

NORMAN
PRICE

BELLA
LASAGNE

JAMES

SARAH

MEET ALL THESE FRIENDS IN BUZZ BOOKS:

Thomas the Tank Engine
The Animals of Farthing Wood
Biker Mice From Mars
James Bond Junior
Fireman Sam
Joshua Jones
Rupert
Babar

First published 1991 by Buzz Books,
an imprint of Reed International Books Ltd
Michelin House, 81 Fulham Road, London SW3 6RB
Reprinted 1992

LONDON MELBOURNE AUCKLAND

Fireman Sam © 1985 Prism Art & Design Ltd

Text © 1991 William Heinemann Ltd
Illustrations © 1991 William Heinemann Ltd
Based on the animation series produced by Bumper Films
for S4C/Channel 4 Wales and Prism Art & Design Ltd.
Original idea by Dave Gingell and Dave Jones,
assisted by Mike Young. Characters created by Rob Lee.
All rights reserved.

ISBN 1 85591 109 4

Printed in Italy by Olivotto

ALL IN A GOOD CAUSE

Story by Caroline Hill-Trevor
Developed from a storyline by Rob Lee
and a script by Nia Ceidiog

Illustrations by The County Studio

Trevor Evans had been installing Bella's new shower and was just finishing reconcreting the pavement outside the cafe.

"There you are, Bella," he said, stepping back to admire his work. "You're going to have the smartest shower in Pontypandy, even if I say so myself."

"Thanks to you, Trevor," Bella replied. "Come in for some dinner when you've finished, on the house."

"Ooo, yes please, Bella!" Trevor called.

"Look at this, Trev," said Fireman Sam. "£300 for the children's ward, all from the fire station raffle." He opened his briefcase.

"How about some raffle tickets?" called out Fireman Sam as he went into the cafe. He put his case down on an old box of rubbish.

"Thanks, Fireman Sam. I'll buy five," replied Bella, dumping some more rubbish on top of the pile. She'd been clearing out while Trevor installed her shower.

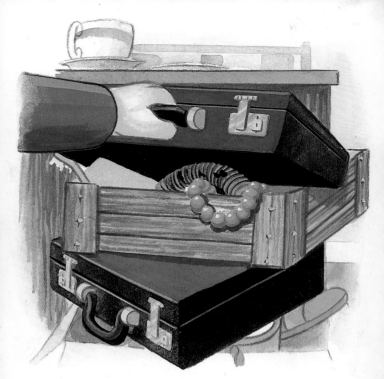

"Thanks, Bella," said Fireman Sam, giving Bella the tickets. "It's all in a good cause. We've raised £300 already." He picked up the case from the top of the boxes and left the cafe.

"Ciao, Fireman Sam," said Bella. She looked down, and frowned at the pile of rubbish. "But I thought . . ."

9

Up at the fire station, Elvis and Penny were admiring a large basket of fruit.

"That looks juicy," said Fireman Sam.

"Yes, Mrs Price has donated it as a raffle prize," Penny explained. "Isn't she kind?"

"Yuk! These are bad," said Elvis, spitting out a grape.

"Trust Dilys," sighed Fireman Sam.

"How's it going, Fireman Sam?" asked Station Officer Steele when he arrived.

"£300 so far, Sir, and we haven't finished yet. Could you look after the money while we do the charity bed push in Pontypandy this afternoon, please?"

"That's the spirit! Keep up the good work, Fireman Sam!" said Station Officer Steele.

"Oi, Mr Evans," said Norman cheekily, popping his head round the corner. "Can I write my name in the wet concrete?"

"Just you dare, Norman Price!" Trevor warned.

"How about a humbug then?" Norman offered Trevor the bag of sweets.

"Don't mind if I do," replied Trevor.
Squelch! He stepped into the wet concrete!

Bella, meanwhile, was piling up her
rubbish in the garden. "Time for a good
bonfire. I don't need all this junk in my new
bathroom – it's no good to anyone," she
thought to herself.

"You can't trust public transport any more," Dilys grumbled as the charity bed push passed the bus stop. Penny rattled the bucket and Dilys dropped in a small coin.

"Seeing as you've paid your fare, Dilys, we'll give you a lift," Penny grinned.

Trevor was still concreting when they arrived outside the shop.

"That looks comfy, Dilys," he called.

"Yes, and it's more reliable than the bus service these days," retorted Dilys. "Thanks for the ride, Penny."

"That's interesting," Dilys thought, taking a good look at the rubbish Bella had heaped up for her bonfire. She poked around and pulled a couple of things out.

"It would be a shame to burn these – I'm sure I could use them."

Checking that no-one was looking, she scurried home.

When Fireman Sam got back to the fire
station, Station Officer Steele looked
worried. Fireman Sam's briefcase was open
on his desk, empty!

"Now, Fireman Sam, where did you last
see the money?" he asked.

"Um . . . oh yes, at Bella's this morning.
She was clearing out rubbish. Quick!"

Bella carried the last load of rubbish outside and set fire to the pile.

"Mamma mia! I didn't know I had so much to throw away," she said as the fire blazed.

She heard the telephone ringing and hurried inside.

"Hello Fireman Sam. Don't worry about the smoke. It's only my bonfire."

"Bella, have you got a briefcase like mine? I think they've got mixed up."

"Zat old thing! I've just put him on the bonfire. Why?"

The line went dead.

19

Elvis and Penny were sitting in the fire station mess when the alarm rang and Fireman Sam charged in.

"There's a fire at the cafe," he shouted.

"Oh don't worry," said Penny, sitting down again. "Bella's having a bonfire, that's all."

"I know," said Fireman Sam, "and the briefcase, with the money for the children's ward inside, is on it!"

Grabbing their helmets, the crew jumped into Jupiter. With the siren blaring and the lights flashing, they roared off down the road towards the cafe.

Watched by Trevor, Jupiter screeched to a halt in the wet concrete outside the cafe. Dragging the hose, the firefighters rushed round the back to the bonfire.

"What's going on at Bella's?" asked Norman, coming out of the shop to watch.

But it was too late. All that was left of the Bella's pile of rubbish were a few smoking remains. And there was no sign of the briefcase!

"Well, that's it," said Fireman Sam. "£300 up in smoke. I'll never repay that."

"As it's for you, Bella, I'll have one last go at this job," Trevor agreed with a weary groan as he looked at the tyre marks in the wet concrete. "But, this is my last try – any more marks will have to stay."

He didn't see Norman grinning as he listened round the corner.

24

"What am I going to do?" groaned
Fireman Sam. "How was I to know that
Bella had a briefcase identical to mine? Now
we'll have to start all over again."

Everyone was silent. Then, they heard
hysterical screaming coming from across
the street.

They raced outside to see Dilys waving her arms about.

"What's wrong Dilys?" Fireman Sam cried, forgetting all about the money as he rushed over to help.

"Nothing . . . but Fireman Sam! Look!"

Dilys was carrying a black briefcase and waving fistfuls of £5 notes!

"That's the raffle ticket money! Thank goodness for that," said Fireman Sam, heaving a sigh of relief. "Where did you find that briefcase?" he smiled.

"Ah, well, I er . . . noticed it on Bella's bonfire and I er . . ." Dilys mumbled, going pink. "Anyway, waste not, want not, I say."

"Too right, Dilys! You're a heroine!"

"That's it – until Bella gets her next new bathroom anyway," said Trevor, exhausted. "Now for some Italian home cooking."

"Go and look at my masterpiece," he said to Fireman Sam and Bella when he'd finished eating.

They all trooped outside.

"Not bad," chuckled Fireman Sam, "but I'm not sure about the hair!"

"What the . . ." Trevor gasped, staring at the cartoon in the pavement. "That Norman gets everywhere!"

FIREMAN SAM

STATION OFFICER
STEELE

TREVOR EVANS

ELVIS
CRIDLINGTON

PENNY MORRIS